To Jill S.—

WITH THANKS FOR HER SUPPORT, GUIDANCE

AND FRIENDSHIP.

PHILOMEL BOOKS

Published by the Penguin Group
Penguin Group (USA) LLC, 375 Hudson Street, New York, NY 10014

USA | Canada | UK | Ireland | Australia | New Zealand | India | South Africa | China
penguin.com
A Penguin Random House Company

Library of Congress Cataloging-in-Publication Data is available upon request.
Manufactured in China by South China Printing Co. Ltd.
ISBN 978-0-399-16093-6
1 3 5 7 9 10 8 6 4 2

Edited by Jill Santopolo.   Design by Semadar Megged.   Text set in 15-point Alinea Incise.
The art was created by using Winsor & Newton watercolors on Lanaquarelle watercolor paper.

Millie Fierce Sleeps out

Jane Manning

PHILOMEL BOOKS
An Imprint of Penguin Group (USA)

Being good wasn't easy.
But Millie knew that being fierce
ruined parties,
and made people mad,
and even made them cry.

So Millie had kept herself
fierce-free all summer long.

Since she'd been such a sugar-pie,
Mom said she could have her
sleep out.
Her gummy-wormy,
scary-movie,
shadow-puppety
sleep-out.

It would be only as far as
her own backyard.
But it felt like it could be
the Outback out there,
or the Amazon jungle,
or maybe even Mars.

She'd planned each detail
as precisely as a portrait.
Her best friend, Maya, was coming.
So was her cousin Lizzie.
And Buddy, too.

Millie and Grandpa pitched the tent
at the very back of the backyard.
They checked the weather
and double-checked the supplies.

Flashlight, gummy worms, lantern: check.
Bug net, sleeping bag, headlamp: check.
Three monster movies
and one zombie movie: check.
S'mores and root beer: check and check.

Millie combed her hair
and gave herself
her sweetest smile.
She'd promised to be nice all night
and had packed her fierceness away
as tightly as a rolled tent.

Nothing, she decided, was going to
ruin her sleep-out.
Not even herself.

Millie was like a jumping bean
in new striped pajamas
waiting for her guests to arrive.

The minute they did,
she hurried them out to camp
as the moon played hide-and-seek
with them
between the trees.
But even though the tent was straight
and the moon was full,
right from the start
things did not go as planned.

Lizzie put her sleeping bag in the wrong place.

And Maya and Buddy ate all but one of the s'mores.

It made Millie's
right eye **twitch**,
but still she smiled
as sweet as sugar.

When Millie made her excellent
shadow puppets on the ceiling
like The Zombie Hand!
and The Grizzly Bear!
Maya and Lizzie were too scared
even to look.

Millie's lip curled into a sour puss,
but she clamped her mouth shut,
then switched off the flashlight
without a hint of fierceness.

Nothing was going to ruin her sleep-out.
Not even a shadow puppet.

And although her nose twisted,
she refused to get fierce
when Maya thought she saw a real spider in the
gummy worms,
then chucked the whole bag out of the tent.
Nothing was going to ruin Millie's sleep-out.
Not even a spider.

Millie didn't get fierce
when no one would explore the
Outback with her.
Or when she sat on sticky burrs.

But she considered it.

And when a cloud slid silently across the moon,
and the first raindrops came
plop-plopping down on the tent,
Millie kept the top on tight
to her inner fierce.
She knew what would happen if it got out.
It would ruin everything.

But then, she heard a growl
just outside the tent.
"Was that a zombie?" asked Lizzie,
her eyes as big as dinner plates.
"It sounds like a bear!" cried Maya
as she dove into her sleeping bag
and zipped it up.

Millie felt both eyes twitch
and her ears sizzle.
Still, she clenched her fists
and forced her fierceness to stay inside.
But then came a snarl
and Maya and Lizzie screamed at once
while Buddy shivered alone.

It looked like something was about to ruin Millie's
sleep-out after all.

Millie's hair frizzed itself into a magnificent tangle.

A puff of hot air blasted from her nose.

She couldn't fight it anymore.

Millie turned FIERCE.

Millie Fierce grabbed her flashlight.
"Even if it's a mountain lion," she sneered,
"or a dragon with bad breath,
it's not going to ruin my sleep-out!"

The Outback was pitch-black,
and in the Amazon, rain poured down.
But Millie Fierce didn't care.
She swept her light around like a lighthouse beacon.
It landed on a growling, snarling,
stooping lump.

It wasn't a zombie.
It wasn't a bear.

It was Vincent,
the pug from next door,
come to gobble down
gummy worms.

Millie Fierce screamed like a samurai,
and Vincent stopped gobbling.

Then she chased him like bad luck.
And Vincent ran back home faster
than he'd ever run in his life.

Then Millie stopped cold,
soaked and moping.
She'd let her fierce out.
And she knew what that meant . . .

But she was wrong!
Tonight it meant a kiss from Buddy,
a hug from Lizzie,
and the last s'more from Maya.
"You saved us!" Lizzie cried.

Millie smiled her widest smile.
She and her fierce self hadn't ruined
her sleep-out.
She'd saved it!

They celebrated by rescuing the gummy worms
and watching *The Creature from Planet X.*
And when Vincent returned and growled again,
Millie growled right back.

Sometimes it takes a little ferocity to set things right.